Copyright © 2020 Clavis Publishing Inc., New York

Originally published as *Aan tafel met Zaza* in Belgium and the Netherlands by Clavis Uitgeverij, 2009
English translation from the Dutch by Clavis Publishing Inc., New York

Visit us on the Web at www.clavis-publishing.com.

Dinnertime for Zaza written and illustrated by Milo Freeman

ISBN 978-1-60537-496-3

This book was printed in February 2020 at Wai Man Book Binding (China) Ltd.
Flat A, 9/F., Phase 1, Kwun Tong Industrial Centre, 472-484 Kwun Tong Road, Kwun Tong, Kowloon, H.K.

First Edition
10 9 8 7 6 5 4 3 2 1

MYLO FREEMAN

Dinnertime for Zaza

Clavis

NEW YORK

Zaza is cooking in her little kitchen.
Mmm, it smells delicious!

"Dinner is ready," Zaza calls to her friends.
There is a place for everyone at the table.

Bobby has to put a bib on.
She can be messy sometimes.
Rosie is ready to dig in.
Pinkie is hungry too.

Mo loves vegetables.
He wants another bite.
"That's the way, Mo.
Vegetables make you strong."

George Giraffe isn't very hungry.

That's okay.

He doesn't have to eat a lot.

"But you have to try a bite of everything!"

Zaza tells him.

"Another bite for Rosie
and one more for Pinkie.
Then we can have dessert."

Here comes Mommy.
"Dinner is ready," she says.

Enjoy your meal, Zaza!